BABY BEAR'S NOT HIBERNATING

Lynn Plourde

ILLUSTRATED BY
Teri Weidner

Down East Books

"I'm staying awake the **WHO-O-O-O-O-OLE** winter," said Baby Black Bear.

"Sure, son." Papa Bear winked.

"Of course you are." Mama Bear grinned.

"I **mean** it!" Baby Bear growled the best growl a baby black bear can growl.

Gr-gr-mmm-mmm!

"Owl, do you hibernate in winter?" asked Baby Bear.

"Certainly **not**," said Owl.

"But how do you stay awake **a-a-a-a-a-all** winter long?"

"I perch in trees and **hoot-hoot-hoot** the time away."

"Really?" said Baby Bear. "I can climb trees. I'm still working on my growling, but hooting can't be that hard. See you around—I'm **not** hibernating."

"Moose, do you hibernate in winter?" asked Baby Bear.

"Nope, not me," said Moose.

"But you're so **big**! What do you eat all winter?"

"Well, I eat everything I can **before** winter— to fatten up. Then when winter comes, I eat just one twig at a time."

"Really?" said Baby Bear. "I have to fatten up before I hibernate so that's not different, and one twig at a time sounds easy enough. See you around— I'm **not** hibernating."

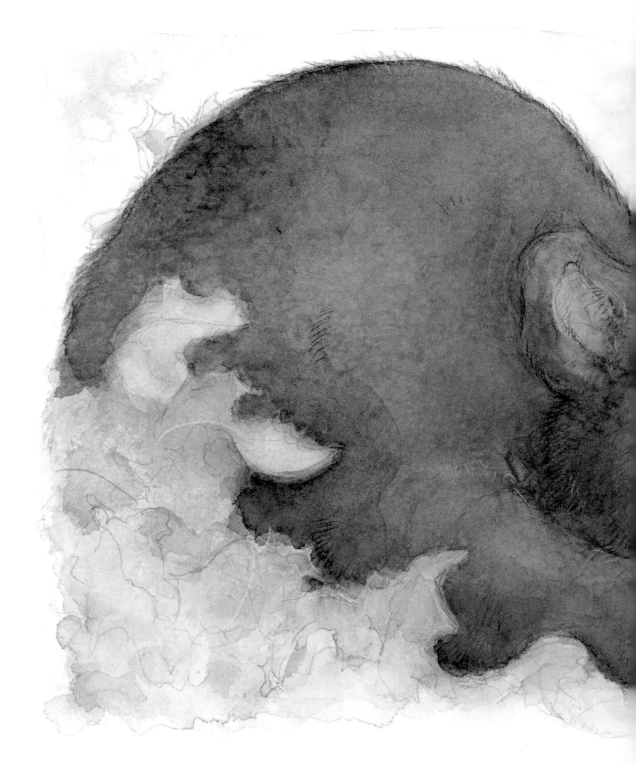

"Hare, do you hibernate in winter?" asked Baby Bear.

"Not me," said Hare.

"But how do you stay warm in the cold and snow?"

"I grow a thick white fur coat."

"Really?" said Baby Bear. "Maybe my fur will grow thick and white if I stay outside all winter. See you around—I'm **not** hibernating."

Baby Bear spent the last few days of fall frolicking until the day it started to snow.

"Winter's early this year," said Papa Bear.

"Time for bed. Let's snuggle 'til spring," said Mama Bear.

"Not me," said Baby Bear. He gave his parents an extra big bear hug and headed outside.

"He'll be back." Papa Bear winked at his wife. "I tried the same thing when I was a cub. You get some rest— I'll keep an eye on him."

The snow fell harder.

"Winter is **fun**!" said Baby Bear.

But when night arrived,
Baby Bear yawned a **big**
yawn.

"Too tired. Mind if I join
you, Owl?" asked Baby
Bear.

"Suit yourself. Just use a
different branch."

Owl went **Hoot-hoot-hoot!**

Baby Bear went **Hoo-Hoo-Zzzzzz—**

Crash!

The next day, Baby Bear's biggest growl came from his belly.

"Too hungry. Mind if I join you, Moose?" asked Baby Bear.

"Mmmm-mmmm-whatever."

Baby Bear munched alongside Moose, one twig at a time.

"**Blech!**" said Baby Bear. "Twigs are too hard!"

"What'd you expect from frozen sticks?" asked Moose.

The next day Baby Bear shivered and quivered as the temperature dropped.

"Too cold. Mind if I join you, Hare?" asked Baby Bear.

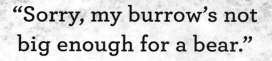

"Sorry, my burrow's not big enough for a bear."

"**Brrrrrrr!**" said Baby Bear. "How long will it take my fur to get thick and white like yours?"

"I'm not sure," said Hare, "but maybe hopping will keep you warm until it does."

So Baby Bear hop-

hop-

hopped until . . .

he dropped.

The snow never stopped.

"Have you seen Baby Bear?" asked Owl.

"Have you seen Baby Bear?" asked Moose.

"He hopped that-a-way,"
said Hare.

"Where?"

"There."

Owl flapped some snow away.

Moose plowed some snow away.

Hare kicked some snow away.

And there was Baby Bear . . .

but he wasn't alone.

"**Shhhhh!** Don't tell him I was here," whispered Papa Bear as he tiptoed toward home.

Owl, Moose, and Hare shook Baby Bear awake.

"Is it spring yet?" asked Baby Bear.

"Not quite," his friends giggled.

"Wow!" said Baby Bear. "I stayed awake almost the **WHO-O-O-O-O-OLE** winter."

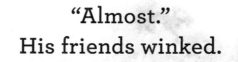
"Almost."
His friends winked.

"I better get home before my parents wake up and get worried about me."

"Good idea," said his friends as they followed
Baby Bear back to his den.

"See you around—in the **spring**," said Owl.

"I'll save you some twigs," said Moose.

"Remember, I'll be brown then," said Hare.

"I'll dream about you, friends," said Baby Bear.

"Just right!" said Baby Bear.

BLACK BEAR FACTS

Names
The scientific name for black bears is *Ursus americanus*. Baby black bears are *cubs*, female adults are *sows*, and male adults are *boars*.

Color
Black bears are always black—right? Wrong! Black bears that live where there are thick forests, such as in Maine, are black. But those that live farther south and west, where there are more fields and fewer trees, are lighter colors, such as brown, cinnamon, or gray.

Weight
Baby black bears weigh only 12 ounces, the weight of a soup can, when they are born. At three months old when they leave the den, they weigh 5 pounds. Then they just keep growing until they weigh from 90 to 600 pounds, with the heaviest male on record weighing 880 pounds!

Food
Black bears are omnivores, which means they eat both plants and meat. They eat fruit, nuts, acorns, grass, and leaves. For meat, they eat insects, fish, and carrion (dead animals). In the fall, black bears spend 20 to 23 hours a day searching for and eating food so as to have enough extra fat on their bodies to make it through hibernation.

Hibernating
Black bears sleep through the winter, but not too deep a sleep. This is called *torpor* when they do not eat, drink, or go to the bathroom, but can wake up if they need to. Black bears hibernate because there is not enough food available in the winter. When mothers give birth to cubs, they wake up enough to lick them clean and nurse them. Cubs hibernate with their mothers a second winter and do not head out on their own until they are two years old.

Growl?
People think black bears growl, but they do not. In forty years of bear watching, people at the North American Bear Center have never heard a black bear growl. Usually they are silent, but may huff if nervous, moan if angry, and cry if hurt or separated from their mother.

FAST FACTS

- Black bears can run 35 miles per hour.

- Black bears are great tree climbers.

- Black bears can live up to 30 years.

- A black bear's sense of smell is 7 times greater than a search dog's.

- A black bear's nose is 100 times bigger than a human's nose.

- Black bears have two coats— underfur to keep them warm and outer hair to keep out bugs and dirt and to repel water.

- Black bears molt or shed their fur every summer and grow new thick coats by fall to keep them warm when they hibernate.

- Female black bears live in a 2-4 square mile territory; males in a 20-100 square mile territory.

With love to Matt,
my fact-loving son-in-law.
—L.P.

For Chris and Nick, with love.
—T.W.

Down East Books

An imprint of Globe Pequot

Distributed by NATIONAL BOOK NETWORK

Story Copyright © 2017 by Lynn Plourde
Illustrations © 2017 by Teri Weidner

Design by Piper Wallis

British Library Cataloguing-in-Publication Information available

Library of Congress Cataloging-in-Publication Data available

ISBN 978-1-60893-622-9 (hardcover)
ISBN 978-1-60893-623-6 (e-book)

♾™ The paper used in this publication meets the minimum requirements of American National Standard for Information Sciences—Permanence of Paper for Printed Library Materials, ANSI/NISO Z39.48-1992.